CASTAWAYS!

KLaSKY
CSUPO INC.

Based on the TV series *Rugrats*® created by Arlene Klasky, Gabor Csupo, and Paul Germain
and *The Wild Thornberrys*® created by Klasky Csupo Inc., as seen on Nickelodeon®.

SIMON SPOTLIGHT
An imprint of Simon & Schuster Children's Publishing Division
1230 Avenue of the Americas, New York, New York 10020
Manufactured in the United States of America
First Edition
2 4 6 8 10 9 7 5 3 1
ISBN 0-689-85471-4

CASTAWAYS!

adapted by Sarah Willson
based on the screenplay by Kate Boutillier
illustrated by Patrick J. Dene, Bradley J. Gake, and Mike Giles

Simon Spotlight/Nickelodeon

New York   London   Toronto   Sydney   Singapore

"Stu must have taken Spike for one more potty run," said Didi, looking around. "He should be back soon."

Everyone was eagerly waiting on the dock. They were all excited to board the world-famous *Lipschitz* cruise ship.

"He'd better come back soon," snapped Drew. "He has all our tickets!"

Tommy, Susie, and the other babies were waiting near the luggage.

"That sure is a nice cambera, Susie," said Tommy.

"Thanks," said Susie. "My mommy and daddy couldn't come along, so they gave it to me to take pictures to show them."

All of a sudden Howard let out an alarmed cry.
"Hey!" he said. "Is it me, or is the dock moving?"
"The ship is sailing without us!" yelled Drew.

Toot-toot! Everyone turned from the departing ship to see a tiny boat chugging toward them. Stu was at the helm.

"Ahoy, mates!" he called heartily. "Climb aboard for seven fun-filled days on the SS *Nancy.* No fancy packaged tour—just the thrill of the open sea, the smell of the salt air, and the joy of close friends and family!"

The grown-ups gaped at the tiny boat in disbelief.

"I can't believe you did this!" said Chas angrily.

"We'll follow the *Lipschitz* cruise ship and board it at the first port," declared Drew.

No sooner had they set sail than the skies opened.
Rain poured down. Thunder boomed. Lightning flashed.
"Everyone get below!" yelled Betty.

A wave crashed over the tiny boat, sending it up into
the air. It landed upside down in the churning waters.
Below deck everything turned topsy-turvy.

Water began pouring in. "Abandon ship!" yelled Stu. "Grab the kids and get out!"
They all bobbed to the surface. "The boat is sinking!" yelled Charlotte.
Suddenly Betty's head and shoulders burst out of the water. "I took a minute to grab a few things I thought might come in handy," she said, grinning. She held up Dil's pacifier and folded-up stroller. Then she pulled on a cord attached to a yellow square under her arm. An inflatable lifeboat sprang open. Everyone jumped in.

The storm passed. Night fell and everyone drifted off to sleep.

Early the next morning the lifeboat jolted to a stop. Everyone woke up.

"Land ho!" said Stu. They had washed up on a sandy beach. The babies and their parents stepped out of the lifeboat. "I know exactly where we are! See? We're on this tiny little island called . . . Uninhabited," said Stu, studying his soggy map.

"Drew!" yelled Charlotte. "The lifeboat is gone!"

"You didn't tie up the lifeboat?" Drew angrily asked Stu.

"I meant to . . . ," said Stu. The lifeboat drifted out to sea.

"We're stranded! With no food!" moaned Howard.

"We need some order here!" barked Betty. "Stu, you keep an eye on the kids. The rest of you, follow me."

The adults built a playpen for the babies. Inside, Tommy got an idea.

"Look! I think it's the topical drain forest—just like we sawed on Nigel Strawberry's telabision show!"

Nigel Thornberry was one of Tommy's heroes.

"I bet if we go in there, we'll find him," said Tommy. "Nigel Strawberry knows all about the great outbores. He can help us get home! Who wants to help me look for him?"

"We all will!" said Susie.

"Not me," said Angelica. "You babies won't last a second in that drain forest!"

But Susie and the babies were already heading toward the forest.

While the other grown-ups followed Betty's orders, Stu began collecting things on the beach. Angelica marched over to him.

"What's all this junk, Uncle Stu?" asked Angelica.

"It's not junk," he replied. "These everyday items can be used to make lots of things . . . like a radio. That's it—I'll build a radio and send a distress signal! Angelica, keep an eye on the babies for a minute, okay?" He hurried away.

"But they went off into the drain forest!" scoffed Angelica. "Spike! Wake up and go get the babies."

Tommy and the babies walked through the dark rain forest. Soon Chuckie needed a break. "I think I need to find a potty," he said, walking toward the trees.

When Chuckie emerged, the others were nowhere to be seen. "Guys? Wait up!" he called.

As Chuckie was looking for the others, he tripped and dove headlong into a muddy puddle.

Chuckie tottered over to a stream to wash the mud off. As he took off his clothes and his glasses he heard a strange sound.

Somebody crept over to Chuckie's clothes and swiped his shorts and shirt. In their place a different pair of shorts appeared. Chuckie felt around blindly and found the shorts, which he put on. "What happened to my shoes and my glasses?" he asked out loud.

A wild-looking boy, who looked a lot like Chuckie, quickly put on Chuckie's clothes, shoes, and glasses. The boy's name was Donnie. He scampered away into the woods.

Chuckie groped his way farther into the forest, in the opposite direction.

Tommy and the other babies were about to go and look for Chuckie, when Donnie appeared—in Chuckie's clothing. Donnie jabbered something.

"Uh, are you okay, Chuckie?" asked Tommy.

Donnie motioned for them to follow, and then bounded away.

"Hey, since when did Chuckie start talking backward?" asked Phil.

Meanwhile Nigel Thornberry was searching nearby for the never-before-photographed clouded leopard. Suddenly at the bottom of the cliff, Donnie appeared with Tommy and the babies. Nigel picked up his binoculars.

"Mr. Strawberry!" yelled Susie.

"What are these babies doing here?" Nigel exclaimed. "Stay there, children! I'm coming down!"

As Nigel started down the cliff he fell and hit his head. He got up, dazed.

"Are you okay, Mr. Strawberry?" asked Susie.

"Why are you calling me 'mister'?" asked Nigel. "I'm only this many years old," he said, extending three fingers. "Do any of you remember where I left my tricycle?"

"Uh, no, Mr. Strawberry," replied Susie. "We're shipwrecked on this island. We was hoping you could help Tommy's daddy."

"Look what I can do!" Nigel shouted, standing on his head. "Oopsie-daisy!"

"Tommy, I think Nigel Strawberry is acting kind of funny," said Susie.

"Maybe he's got diapie rash," said Lil.

Not far away Tommy's dog, Spike, was sniffing around, searching frantically for the missing babies. Spike nearly stumbled over a girl who sat listening to the chattering of a chimp. The girl and the chimp both looked up at Spike in surprise.

"Uh, hi!" said the girl to Spike. "I'm Eliza Thornberry." Eliza could talk to animals. "Are you looking for something?"

"Yeah," said Spike. "I'm looking for my babies, but I can't find them anywhere."

"Don't worry," said Eliza. "We'll help you look for them."

Suddenly a leopard sprang in front of them.
"Oh, my!" exclaimed Eliza. "You're a . . ."
"I'm Siri, the clouded leopard," said Siri.
"I'm Spike, the purebred mutt!" joked Spike.
"Look at my claws," hissed Siri.
Darwin screamed.

"I don't have time for this," said Spike. "I have to find my babies."

"Babies? Alone in the forest?" inquired Siri.

"Yes, they are my human babies," answered Spike.

Siri immediately ran off into the forest.

"Spike!" cried Eliza. "Siri's going after the babies! Hurry—we have to find my parents!"

They ran as fast as they could through the forest.

Nearby Angelica also happened to be heading in the direction of the Thornberrys' camp. She arrived at a clearing and rubbed her eyes at what she saw.

Debbie Thornberry was sunning herself on a lounge chair.

Angelica marched over to her. "Hey, lady!" she said.

Debbie pulled off her sunglasses and stared at Angelica. "Huh? This island is supposed to be deserted!" she said.

"Yeah, whatever. I'm, uh, Angeli-tiki, a native island princess." She walked over to the Commvee and then all around it. "Nice wheels," Angelica said.

Angelica opened the Commvee door and went inside. She walked over to a little submarine. "What's this bubble thing?" she asked.

"It's called a 'bathysphere,'" Debbie called out. "It can travel underwater."

Angelica picked up a pair of binoculars and looked into the forest. "Those dumb babies are standing on top of a mountain! I'm going to be blamed for not baby-sitting them! Can you drive me to my, er, native village?" she asked Debbie. "I hafta go now!"

"I guess Mom would understand, since it's a native thing," Debbie said, shrugging. She slid into the driver's seat. They buckled up and started off.

While Debbie drove the Commvee down the beach, Eliza, Darwin, and Spike raced out of the forest. As Debbie swerved to miss hitting them the Commvee spun out of control and landed in the lagoon.

"Debbie! There's a bunch of lost babies out here, and a leopard's after them!" yelled Eliza.

"I gotta get out of here!" said Angelica. "If those babies get hurt, I'll be in big trouble!"

Angelica made her way to the bathysphere. As she started it up it veered out of control, hitting the Commvee and creating a hole in its side. Water poured in, and everything floated out of the windows.

"My stuff!" cried Debbie.

Angelica pulled a lever and the bathysphere disappeared underwater.

Meanwhile on a nearby hill, Susie and the babies were playing follow-the-leader with Nigel. Suddenly they heard a growl. Siri was slinking toward them, her teeth bared.

"Uh-oh. It's a giant kitty cat with big teeths!" said Tommy.

Donnie took Dil out of the stroller and waved the empty stroller in front of Siri. Then Donnie jabbered to Siri.

"He's so brave!" said Lil.

"Climb on!" yelled Tommy, pointing to the stroller. Nigel and the babies piled on. Then Donnie gave the stroller a big push and jumped on last.

The stroller rolled down the
hill, and Siri ran after it.

Donnie jumped off the stroller and came
face-to-face with Chuckie.
"I want my clothes back!" said Chuckie.
Donnie led Chuckie into some bushes.
When they emerged, they were wearing
their own clothes.

"That's better," said Chuckie, adjusting his glasses. "Now I can see, and—" Chuckie gasped as he saw Siri.

Donnie quickly grabbed a palm frond and put Chuckie on it. Then he gave Chuckie a good push. Chuckie flew down the hill as Siri chased him.

"Come on, Chuckie! Hurry!" yelled the babies.

Tommy grabbed Chuckie and pulled him into the stroller. Susie managed to snap a picture in all the confusion. When Donnie saw that the babies were safe, he took off through the rain forest.

The stroller rolled into a cave, and the babies flew out of it and into a tunnel. They slid down a twisting waterslide and finally arrived at an underground lake.

"That's Nigel Strawberry!" said Chuckie, amazed.

"Tommy, I'm not sure Nigel Strawberry can help us get home," said Susie.

"I thought he was the bestest nature explorer ever," Tommy said sadly.

Then something popped out of the water. It was the bathysphere!

"Adoy, babies!" called Angelica. "Hop in!"

Back at the beach Marianne found the babies' parents.

"Look, Deed!" said Stu as he ran up to them. "I've built a radio from a coconut!"

"But where are the kids?" Didi cried.

"Oh, don't worry, honey. Angelica's watching them," said Stu.

As Eliza, Debbie, and Darwin joined the adults on the beach they heard the children's voices through the radio. While Debbie told everyone that the Commvee had sunk, the bathysphere, with Angelica at the wheel, went whizzing by them and out toward the ocean.

Marianne used Stu's coconut radio to try and talk to the babies. She realized that Nigel was in the bathysphere too, and heard him babbling.

"Something's wrong with Nigel," said Marianne to the rest of the group.

Inside the bathysphere the dials were blinking ominously. All of a sudden the bathysphere plunged downward. Nigel fell backward, knocked his head, and was out cold.

Tommy pulled out his emergency bottle and squirted some milk in Nigel's face. Nigel sputtered and opened his eyes. "I say! Who are all these adorable children? Hmm," Nigel said, stroking his chin. "I have no idea of our coordinates, and we're nearly out of air."

"Nigel," said Marianne through the radio. "Can you bring the bathysphere to the surface?"

"That's impossible at the moment, dearest," replied Nigel. "You need to engage the automatic retrieval system in the Commvee."

While Nigel assured the babies that everything was going to be okay, Marianne, Eliza, and the other adults set out to raise the Commvee. With some teamwork they were finally able to fix the gash in the side and raise her up.

"We're on our way!" said Marianne to Nigel.

Through the radio, the babies heard their parents cheer.

"We shall have you in your parents' arms in just a jiffy," Nigel said to the babies. The bathysphere began to rise.

Later that evening, after the babies were reunited with their parents, everyone relaxed while having dinner on the roof of the Commvee. The *Lipschitz* cruise ship towed the Commvee through the ocean. Nigel beamed when he found the picture of the leopard that Susie had taken.

"I'm going to miss our island," said Chas.
Didi proposed a toast. "To the best vacation we ever had!"
"To Stu!" said everyone.

The babies, meanwhile, ate cookies and drank juice.

"Well, guys. We did it!" said Tommy. "We found Nigel Strawberry and no one's mad anymores."

"Pickles, you may grow up to be just like Nigel Strawberry after all," said Angelica.

"Thanks, Angelica," said Tommy. "But I think I'll grow up to be just like my daddy."